POET

C0-AQI-722

6/6

7 50

HELEN OF TROY
AND OTHER POEMS

By SARA TEASDALE

HELEN OF TROY AND OTHER
POEMS, 1911

RIVERS TO THE SEA, 1915

LOVE SONGS, 1917

FLAME AND SHADOW, 1921

HELEN OF TROY

AND OTHER POEMS

BY

SARA TEASDALE

New York

THE MACMILLAN COMPANY

1931

COPYRIGHT, 1911,
BY SARA TEASDALE.

COPYRIGHT, 1922,
BY THE MACMILLAN COMPANY.

All rights reserved—no part of this book may be reproduced
in any form without permission in writing
from the publisher.

Published October, 1911, reprinted October, 1912.
New and revised edition March, 1922.
Reprinted September, 1926.
"   May, 1931.

Printed in the United States of America by
J. J. LITTLE AND IVES COMPANY, NEW YORK

To

MARION CUMMINGS STANLEY

Thanks are due to the editors of *Harper's, Century, Scribner's,* and other periodicals, for their courteous permission to reprint many of the following poems.

CONTENTS

[ix]

CONTENTS

CONTENTS

[xi]

CONTENTS

HELEN OF TROY
AND OTHER POEMS

HELEN OF TROY

WILD flight on flight against the fading dawn
The flames' red wings soar upward duskily.
This is the funeral pyre and Troy is dead
That sparkled so the day I saw it first,
And darkened slowly after. I am she
Who loves all beauty—yet I wither it.
Why have the high gods made me wreak their wrath—
Forever since my maidenhood to sow
Sorrow and blood about me? See, they keep
Their bitter care above me even now.
It was the gods who led me to this lair,
That though the burning winds should make me
     weak,
They should not snatch the life from out my lips.
Olympus let the other women die;
They shall be quiet when the day is done
And have no care to-morrow. Yet for me
There is no rest. The gods are not so kind
To her made half immortal like themselves.

It is to you I owe the cruel gift,
Leda, my mother, and the Swan, my sire,
To you the beauty and to you the bale;
For never woman born of man and maid

Had wrought such havoc on the earth as I,
Or troubled heaven with a sea of flame
That climbed to touch the silent whirling stars,
Blotting their brightness out before the dawn.
Have I not made the world to weep enough?
Give death to me.

              Yet life is more than death;
How could I leave the sound of singing winds,
The strong clean scent that breathes from off the sea,
Or shut my eyes forever to the spring?
I will not give the grave my hands to hold,
My shining hair to light oblivion.
Have those who wander through the ways of death,
The still wan fields Elysian, any love
To lift their breasts with longing, any lips
To thirst against the quiver of a kiss?
I shall live on to conquer Greece again,
To make the people love, who hate me now.
My dreams are over, I have ceased to cry
Against the fate that made men love my mouth
And left their spirits all too deaf to hear
The songs that echoed always in my soul.

I have no anger now. The dreams are done;
Yet since the Greeks and Trojans would not see
Aught but my body's fairness, till the end,
In all the islands set in all the seas,
And all the lands that lie beneath the sun,
Till light turn darkness, and till time shall sleep,
Men's lives shall waste with longing after me,

HELEN OF TROY

For I shall be the sum of their desire,
The whole of beauty, never seen again.
And they shall stretch their arms and starting, wake,
With "Helen!" on their lips, and in their eyes
The vision of me.   Always I shall be
Limned on the darkness like a shaft of light
That glimmers and is gone.   They shall behold
Each one his dream that fashions me anew;—
With hair like lakes that glint beneath the stars
Dark as sweet midnight, or with hair aglow
Like burnished gold that still retains the fire.
I shall be haunting till the dusk of time
The heavy eyelids that are filled with dreams.

I wait for one who comes with sword to slay—
The king I wronged who searches for me now;
And yet he shall not slay me.   I shall stand
With lifted head and look into his eyes,
Baring my breast to him and to the sun.
He shall not have the power to stain with blood
That whiteness—for the thirsty sword shall fall
And he shall cry and catch me in his arms.
I shall go back to Sparta on his breast.
I shall live on to conquer Greece again!

BEATRICE

SEND out the singers—let the room be still;
They have not eased my pain nor brought me
    sleep.
Close out the sun, for I would have it dark
That I may feel how black the grave will be.
The sun is setting, for the light is red,
And you are outlined in a golden fire,
Like Ursula upon an altar-screen.
Come, leave the light and sit beside my bed,
For I have had enough of saints and prayers.
Strange broken thoughts are beating in my brain,
They come and vanish and again they come.
It is the fever driving out my soul,
And Death stands waiting by the arras there.

Ornella, I will speak, for soon my lips
Shall keep a silence till the end of time.
You have a mouth for loving—listen then:
Keep tryst with Love before Death comes to tryst;
For I, who die, could wish that I had lived
A little closer to the world of men,
Not watching always through the blazoned panes
That show the world in chilly greens and blues
And grudge the sunshine that would enter in.

BEATRICE

I was no part of all the troubled crowd
That moved beneath the palace windows here,
And yet sometimes a knight in shining steel
Would pass and catch the gleaming of my hair,
And wave a mailèd hand and smile at me.
I made no sign to him and turned away,
Frightened and yet glad and full of dreams.
Ah, dreams and dreams that asked no answering!
I should have wrought to make my dreams come true.
But all my life was like an autumn day,
Full of gray quiet and a hazy peace.

What was I saying? All is gone again.
It seemed but now I was the little child
Who played within a garden long ago.
Beyond the walls the festal trumpets blared.
Perhaps they carried some Madonna by
With tossing ensigns in a sea of flowers,
A painted Virgin with a painted Child,
Who saw for once the sweetness of the sun
Before they shut her in an altar-niche
Where tapers smoke against the windy gloom.
I gathered roses redder than my gown
And played that I was Saint Elizabeth,
Whose wine had turned to roses in her hands.
And as I played, a child came through the gate,
A boy who looked at me without a word,
As though he saw stretch far behind my head,
Long lines of radiant angels, row on row.
That day we spoke a little, timidly,

BEATRICE

And after that I never heard his voice;
Never again in after years his voice
That sang so many songs for love of me.
He was content to stand and watch me pass,
To seek for me at matins every day,
Where I could feel his eyes, although I prayed.
I think if he had stretched his hands to me,
Or moved his lips to say a single word,
I might have loved him . . . .

Ornella, are you there? I cannot see—
Is every one so lonely when he dies?

The room is filled with lights—with waving lights—
Who are the men and women 'round the bed?
What have I said, Ornella? Have they heard?
There was no evil hidden in my life,
And yet, oh never, never let them know—

Am I not floating in a mist of light?
Oh, lift me up and I shall reach the sun!

SAPPHO

I have a fair daughter with a form like a golden flower,
Cleïs, the beloved.
                                        Sapphic fragment.

THE twilight's inner flame grows blue and deep,
And in my Lesbos, over leagues of sea,
The temples glimmer moonwise in the trees.
Twilight has veiled the little flower face
Here on my heart, but still the night is kind
And leaves her warm sweet weight against my breast.
Am I that Sappho who would run at dusk
Along the surges creeping up the shore
When tides came in to ease the hungry beach,
And running, running, till the night was black,
Would fall forespent upon the chilly sand
And quiver with the wind from off the sea?
Ah, quietly the shingle waits the tides
Whose waves are stinging kisses, but to me
Love brought no peace, nor darkness any rest.
I crept and touched the foam with feverish hands,
And cried to Love, from whom the sea is sweet,
From whom the sea is bitterer than death.

Ah, Aphrodite, if I sing no more
To thee, God's daughter, powerful as God,

[21]

SAPPHO

It is that thou hast made my life too sweet
To hold the added sweetness of a song.
There is a quiet at the heart of love,
And I have pierced the pain and come to peace.
I hold my peace, my Cleïs, on my heart;
And softer than a little wild bird's wing
Are kisses that she pours upon my mouth.

Ah, never any more when spring like fire
Will flicker in the newly opened leaves,
Shall I steal forth to seek for solitude
Beyond the lure of light Alcæus' lyre,
Beyond the sob that stilled Erinna's voice.
Ah, never with a throat that aches with song,
Beneath the white uncaring sky of spring,
Shall I go forth to hide awhile from Love
The quiver and the crying of my heart.
Still I remember how I strove to flee
The love-note of the birds, and bowed my head
To hurry faster, but upon the ground
I saw two wingèd shadows side by side,
And all the world's spring passion stifled me.

Ah, Love, there is no fleeing from thy might,
No lonely place where thou hast never trod,
No desert thou hast left uncarpeted
With flowers that spring beneath thy warm, quick
    feet.
In many guises didst thou come to me;
I saw thee by the maidens while they danced,

[22]

SAPPHO

Phaon allured me with a look of thine,
In Anactoria I knew thy passion,
I looked at Cercolas and saw thine eyes;
But never wholly, soul and body mine,
Didst thou bid any love me as I loved.
Now I have found the peace that fled from me;
Close, close, against my heart I hold my world.

Ah, Love that made my life a singing cry,
Ah, Love that tuned my lips to lyres of thine,
I taught the world thy music, now alone
I sing for one who falls asleep to hear.

MARIANNA ALCOFORANDO

(The Portuguese Nun—1640-1723)

THE sparrows wake beneath the convent eaves;
I think I have not slept the whole night through.
But I am old; the agèd scarcely know
The times they wake and sleep, for life burns down;
They breathe the calm of death before they die.
The long night ends, the day comes creeping in,
Showing the sorrows that the darkness hid,
The bended head of Christ, the blood, the thorns,
The wall's gray stains of damp, the pallet bed
Where little Sister Marta dreams of saints,
Waking with arms outstretched imploringly
That seek to stay a vision's vanishing.

I never had a vision, yet for me
Our Lady smiled while all the convent slept
One winter midnight hushed around with snow—
I thought she might be kinder than the rest,
And so I came to kneel before her feet,
Sick with love's sorrow and love's bitterness.
But when I would have made the blessèd sign,
I found the water frozen in the font,
And touched sharp ice within the curving stone.
The saints had hid themselves away from me,

MARIANNA ALCOFORANDO

And left the windows black against the night;
And when I sank upon the altar steps,
Before the Virgin Mother and her Child,
The last, pale, low-burnt taper flickered out,
But in the darkness, smooth and fathomless,
Still like a star the holy lamp was twinkling
That cast a dusky glow upon her face.
Then through the numbing cold, peace fell on me,
Submission and the gracious gift of tears,
For when I looked, Oh! blessèd miracle,
Her lips had parted and Our Lady smiled!
And then I knew that Love is worth its pain
And that my heart was richer for his sake,
Since lack of love is bitterest of all.

The day is broad awake—the first long beam
Of level sun finds Sister Marta's face,
And trembling there it lights a timid smile
Upon the lips that say so many prayers,
And have no words for hate and none for love.
But when she passes where her prayers have gone,
Will God not smile a little sadly then,
And send her back with gentle words to earth
That she may hold a child against her breast
And feel its small, warm hands upon her hair?

We weep before the blessèd Mother's shrine,
To think upon her sorrows, but her joys
What nun could ever know a tithing of?
The precious hours she watched above His sleep

MARIANNA ALCOFORANDO

Were worth the fearful anguish of the end;
Yes, lack of love is bitterest of all.
Yet I have felt what thing it is to know
One thought forever, sleeping or awake;
To say one name whose sweetness grows so wild
That it might work a spell on those who weep;
To feel the weight of love upon my heart
So heavy that the blood can scarcely flow.

Love comes to some unlooked-for, quietly,
As when at twilight, with a soft surprise,
We see the new-born crescent in the blue;
And unto others love is planet-like,
A cold and placid gleam that never wavers;
And there are those who wait the call of love
Expectant of his coming, as we watch
To see the east grow pale before the moon
Lifts up her flower-like head against the night.
But love, for me, was like a cruel sun,
That on some rain-drenched morning, when the leaves
Are bowed beneath their clinging weight of drops,
Tears through the mist, and burns with fervent heat
The tender grasses and the meadow flowers;
Then suddenly the heavy clouds close in
And through the dark the thunder's muttering
Is drowned amid the dashing of the rain.

But I have seen my day grow calm again.
The sun sets slowly on a peaceful world,
And sheds a quiet light across the fields.

[26]

GUENEVERE

I was a queen, and I have lost my crown;
A wife, and I have broken all my vows;
A lover, and I ruined him I loved:—
There is no other havoc left to do.
A little month ago I was a queen,
And mothers held their babies up to see
When I came riding out of Camelot.
The women smiled, and all the world smiled too.
And now, what woman's eyes would smile on me?
I am still beautiful, and yet what child
Would think of me as some high, heaven-sent thing,
An angel, clad in gold and miniver?
The world would run from me, and yet I am
No different from the queen they used to love.
If water, flowing silver over stones,
Is forded, and beneath the horses' feet
Grows turbid suddenly, it clears again,
And men will drink it with no thought of harm.
Yet I am branded for a single fault.

I was the flower amid a toiling world,
Where people smiled to see one happy thing,
And they were proud and glad to raise me high;
They only asked that I should be right fair,

GUENEVERE

A little kind, and gownèd wondrously,
And surely it were little praise to me
If I had pleased them well throughout my life.

I was a queen, the daughter of a king.
The crown was never heavy on my head,
It was my right, and was a part of me.
The women thought me proud, the men were kind,
And bowed down gallantly to kiss my hand,
And watched me as I passed them calmly by,
Along the halls I shall not tread again.
What if, to-night, I should revisit them?
The warders at the gates, the kitchen-maids,
The very beggars would stand off from me,
And I, their queen, would climb the stairs alone,
Pass through the banquet-hall, a hated thing,
And seek my chambers for a hiding-place,
And I should find them but a sepulchre,
The very rushes rotted on the floors,
The fire in ashes on the freezing hearth.

I was a queen, and he who loved me best
Made me a woman for a night and day,
And now I go unqueened forevermore.

A queen should never dream on summer nights,
When hovering spells are heavy in the dusk:—
I think no night was ever quite so still,
So smoothly lit with red along the west,
So deeply hushed with quiet through and through.

GUENEVERE

And strangely clear, and sharply dyed with light,
The trees stood straight against a paling sky,
With Venus burning lamp-like in the west.

I walked alone among a thousand flowers,
That drooped their heads and drowsed beneath the
    dew,
And all my thoughts were quieted to sleep.
Behind me, on the walk, I heard a step—
I did not know my heart could tell his tread,
I did not know I loved him till that hour.
The garden reeled a little, I was weak,
And in my breast I felt a wild, sick pain.
Quickly he came behind me, caught my arms,
That ached beneath his touch; and then I swayed,
My head fell backward and I saw his face.

All this grows bitter that was once so sweet,
And many mouths must drain the dregs of it,
But none will pity me, nor pity him
Whom Love so lashed, and with such cruel thongs.

ERINNA

THEY sent you in to say farewell to me,
No, do not shake your head; I see your eyes
That shine with tears. Sappho, you saw the sun
Just now when you came hither; and again,
When you have left me, all the shimmering
Great meadows will laugh lightly, and the sun
Put round about you warm invisible arms
As might a lover, decking you with light.
I go toward darkness though I lie so still.
If I could see the sun, I should look up
And drink the light until my eyes were blind;
I should kneel down and kiss the blades of grass,
And I should call the birds with such a voice,
With such a longing, tremulous and keen,
That they would fly to me and on the breast
Bear evermore to tree-tops and to fields
The kiss I gave them.

            Sappho, tell me this,
Was I not sometimes fair? My eyes, my mouth,
My hair that loved the wind, were they not worth
The breath of love upon them? Yet he passed,
And he will pass to-night when all the air
Is blue with twilight; but I shall not see.

ERINNA

I shall have gone forever. Hold my hands,
Hold fast that Death may never come between;
Swear by the gods you will not let me go;
Make songs for Death as you would sing to Love—
But you will not assuage him. He alone
Of all the gods will take no gifts from men.
I am afraid, afraid.

       Sappho, lean down.
Last night the fever gave a dream to me,
It takes my life and gives me only a dream.
I thought I saw him stand, the man I love,
Here in my quiet chamber, with his eyes
Fixed on me as I entered, while he drew
Silently toward me—he who night by night
Goes by my door without a thought of me—
Neared me and put his hand behind my head,
And leaning toward me, kissed me on the mouth.
That was a little dream for Death to give,
Too short to take the whole of life for, yet
I woke with lips made quiet by a kiss.

The dream is worth the dying. Do not smile
So sadly on me with your shining eyes,
You who can set your sorrow to a song
And ease your hurt by singing. But to me
My songs are less than sea-sand that the wind
Drives stinging over me and bears away.
I have no care what place the grains may fall,
Nor of my songs, if Time shall blow them back,
As land-wind breaks the lines of dying foam

ERINNA

Along the bright wet beaches, scattering
The flakes once more against the laboring sea,
Into oblivion. What do I care
To please Apollo since Love does not hear?
Your words will live forever, men will say
"She was the perfect lover"—I shall die,
I loved too much to live. Go Sappho, go—
I hate your hands that beat so full of life,
Go, lest my hatred hurt you. I shall die,
But you will live to love and love again.
He might have loved some other spring than this;
I should have kept my life—I let it go.
He would not love me now though Cypris bound
Her girdle round me. I am Death's, not Love's
Go from me, Sappho, back to find the sun.

I am alone, alone. O Cyprian . . .

LOVE SONGS

SONG

You bound strong sandals on my feet,
  You gave me bread and wine,
And sent me under sun and stars,
  For all the world was mine.

Oh take the sandals off my feet,
  You know not what you do;
For all my world is in your arms,
  My sun and stars are you.

THE ROSE AND THE BEE

IF I were a bee and you were a rose,
Would you let me in when the gray wind blows?
Would you hold your petals wide apart,
Would you let me in to find your heart,
  If you were a rose?

"If I were a rose and you were a bee,
You should never go when you came to me,
I should hold my love on my heart at last,
I should close my leaves and keep you fast,
  If you were a bee."

THE SONG MAKER

I MADE a hundred little songs
    That told the joy and pain of love,
And sang them blithely, though I knew
    Nothing thereof.

I was a weaver deaf and blind;
    A miracle was wrought for me,
But I have lost my skill to weave
    Since I can see.

For while I sang—oh swift and strange!
    Love passed and touched me on the brow,
And I who made so many songs
    Am silent now.

WILD ASTERS

In the spring I asked the daisies
    If his words were true,
And the clever little daisies
    Always knew.

Now the fields are brown and barren,
    Bitter autumn blows,
And of all the stupid asters
    Not one knows.

WHEN LOVE GOES

I

O MOTHER, I am sick of love,
  I cannot laugh nor lift my head,
My bitter dreams have broken me,
  I would my love were dead.

"Drink of the draught I brew for thee,
Thou shalt have quiet in its stead."

II

Where is the silver in the rain,
  Where is the music in the sea,
Where is the bird that sang all day
  To break my heart with melody?

"The night thou badst Love fly away,
He hid them all from thee."

THE PRINCESS IN THE TOWER

I

THE Princess sings:

I am the princess up in the tower,
   And I dream the whole day through
Of a knight who shall come with a silver spear
   And a waving plume of blue.

I am the princess up in the tower,
   And I dream my dreams by day,
But sometimes I wake, and my eyes are wet,
   When the dusk is deep and gray.

For the peasant lovers go by beneath,
   I hear them laugh and kiss,
And I forget my day-dream knight,
   And long for a love like this.

II

The Minstrel sings:

I lie beside the princess' tower,
   So close she cannot see my face,
And watch her dreaming all day long,
   And bending with a lily's grace.

[40]

THE PRINCESS IN THE TOWER

Her cheeks are paler than the moon
   That sails along a sunny sky,
And yet her silent mouth is red
   Where tender words and kisses lie.

I am a minstrel with a harp,
   For love of her my songs are sweet,
And yet I dare not lift the voice
   That lies so far beneath her feet.

III

The Knight sings:

O princess, cease your dreams awhile
   And look adown your tower's gray side—
The princess gazes far away,
   Nor hears nor heeds the words I cried.

Perchance my heart was overbold,
   God made her dreams too pure to break,
She sees the angels in the air
   Fly to and fro for Mary's sake.

Farewell, I mount and go my way,
   —But oh her hair the sun sifts through—
The tilts and tourneys wait my spear,
   I am the Knight of the Plume of Blue.

WHEN LOVE WAS BORN

WHEN Love was born I think he lay
    Right warm on Venus' breast,
And whiles he smiled and whiles would play
    And whiles would take his rest.

But always, folded out of sight,
    The wings were growing strong
That were to bear him off in flight
    Erelong, erelong.

THE SHRINE

THERE is no Lord within my heart,
Left silent as an empty shrine
Where rose and myrtle intertwine,
Within a place apart.

No god is there of carven stone
To watch with still approving eyes
My thoughts like steady incense rise;
I dream and weep alone.

But if I keep my altar fair,
Some morning I shall lift my head
From roses deftly garlanded
To find the god is there.

THE BLIND

THE birds are all a-building,
   They say the world's a-flower,
And still I linger lonely
   Within a barren bower.

I weave a web of fancies
   Of tears and darkness spun.
How shall I sing of sunlight
   Who never saw the sun?

I hear the pipes a-blowing,
   But yet I may not dance,
I know that Love is passing,
   I cannot catch his glance.

And if his voice should call me
   And I with groping dim
Should reach his place of calling
   And stretch my arms to him,

The wind would blow between my hands
   For Joy that I shall miss,
The rain would fall upon my mouth
   That his will never kiss.

LOVE ME

Brown-thrush singing all day long
  In the leaves above me,
Take my love this April song,
  "Love me, love me, love me!"

When he harkens what you say,
  Bid him, lest he miss me,
Leave his work or leave his play,
  And kiss me, kiss me, kiss me!

THE SONG FOR COLIN

I SANG a song at dusking time
  Beneath the evening star,
And Terence left his latest rhyme
  To answer from afar.

Pierrot laid down his lute to weep,
  And sighed, "She sings for me,"
But Colin slept a careless sleep
  Beneath an apple tree.

FOUR WINDS

"Four winds blowing through the sky,
You have seen poor maidens die,
Tell me then what I shall do
That my lover may be true."
Said the wind from out the south,
"Lay no kiss upon his mouth,"
And the wind from out the west,
"Wound the heart within his breast,"
And the wind from out the east,
"Send him empty from the feast,"
And the wind from out the north,
"In the tempest thrust him forth,
When thou art more cruel than he,
Then will Love be kind to thee."

DEW

I DREAM that he is mine,
  I dream that he is true,
And all his words I keep
  As rose-leaves hold the dew.

O little thirsty rose,
  O little heart beware,
Lest you should hope to hold
  A hundred roses' share.

A MAIDEN

Oh if I were the velvet rose
　Upon the red rose vine,
I'd climb to touch his window
　And make his casement fine.

And if I were the bright-eyed bird
　That twitters on the tree,
All day I'd sing my love for him
　Till he should harken me.

But since I am a maiden
　I go with downcast eyes,
And he will never hear the songs
　That he has turned to sighs.

And since I am a maiden
　My love will never know
That I could kiss him with a mouth
　More red than roses blow.

"I LOVE YOU"

WHEN April bends above me
And finds me fast asleep,
Dust need not keep the secret
A live heart died to keep.

When April tells the thrushes,
The meadow-larks will know,
And pipe the three words lightly
To all the winds that blow.

Above his roof the swallows,
In notes like far-blown rain,
Will tell the chirping sparrow
Beside his window-pane.

O sparrow, little sparrow,
When I am fast asleep,
Then tell my love the secret
That I have died to keep.

BUT NOT TO ME

The April night is still and sweet
  With flowers on every tree;
Peace comes to them on quiet feet,
  But not to me.

My peace is hidden in his breast
  Where I shall never be,
Love comes to-night to all the rest,
  But not to me.

HIDDEN LOVE

I HID the love within my heart,
  And lit the laughter in my eyes,
That when we meet he may not know
  My love that never dies.

But sometimes when he dreams at night
  Of fragrant forests green and dim,
It may be that my love crept out
  And brought the dream to him.

And sometimes when his heart is sick
  And suddenly grows well again,
It may be that my love was there
  To free his life of pain.

SNOW SONG

Fairy snow, fairy snow,
Blowing, blowing everywhere,
  Would that I
  Too, could fly
Lightly, lightly through the air.

Like a small crystal star
I should drift, I should blow
  Near, more near,
  To my dear
Where he comes through the snow.

I should fly to my love
Like a flake in the storm,
  I should die,
  I should die,
On his lips that are warm.

YOUTH AND THE PILGRIM

GRAY pilgrim, you have journeyed far,
    Swear on my sword to me,
Is there a land where Love is not,
    By shore of any sea?

For I am weary of the god,
    And I would flee from him
Though I must take a ship and go
    Beyond the ocean's rim.

"There is a place where Love is not,
    But never a ship leaves land
Can carry you so quickly there
    As the sharp sword in your hand."

THE WANDERER

I saw the sunset-colored sands,
  The Nile like flowing fire between,
  Where Rameses stares forth serene,
And Ammon's heavy temple stands.

I saw the rocks where long ago,
  Above the sea that cries and breaks,
  Bright Perseus with Medusa's snakes
Set free the maiden white like snow.

And many skies have covered me,
  And many winds have blown me forth,
  And I have loved the green bright north,
And I have loved the cold sweet sea.

But what to me are north and south,
  And what the lure of many lands,
  Since you have leaned to catch my hands
And lay a kiss upon my mouth.

I WOULD LIVE IN YOUR LOVE

I WOULD live in your love as the sea-grasses live in
    the sea,
Borne up by each wave as it passes, drawn down
    by each wave that recedes;
I would empty my mind of the dreams that have
    gathered in me,
I would beat with your heart as it beats, I would
    follow your soul as it leads.

MAY

THE wind is tossing the lilacs,
  The new leaves laugh in the sun,
And the petals fall on the orchard wall,
  But for me the spring is done.

Beneath the apple blossoms
  I go a wintry way,
For love that smiled in April
  Is false to me in May.

LESS THAN THE CLOUD TO THE WIND

Less than the cloud to the wind,
  Less than the foam to the sea,
Less than the rose to the storm
  Am I to thee.

More than the star to the night,
  More than the rain to the tree,
More than heaven to earth
  Art thou to me.

BURIED LOVE

I SHALL bury my Love at last
    Beneath a tree,
In the forest tall and black
    Where none can see.

I shall put no flowers at his head,
    Nor stone at his feet,
For the mouth I loved so much
    Was bittersweet.

I shall go no more to his grave,
    For the woods are cold;
I shall gather as much of joy
    As my hands can hold.

I shall stay all day in the sun
    Where the wide winds blow,
But, oh, I shall weep at night
    When none will know.

SONG

O woe is me, my heart is sad,
  For I should never know
If Love came by like any lad,
  Without his silver bow.

Or if he left his arrows sharp
  And came a minstrel weary,
I'd never tell him by his harp
  Nor know him for my dearie.

"O go your ways and have no fear,
  For though Love passes by,
He'll come again a hundred times,
  Before your turn to die."

PIERROT

PIERROT stands in the garden
 Beneath a waning moon,
And on his lute he fashions
 A fragile silver tune.

Pierrot plays in the garden,
 He thinks he plays for me,
But I am quite forgotten
 Under the cherry tree.

Pierrot plays in the garden,
 And all the roses know
That Pierrot loves his music,
 But I love Pierrot.

AT NIGHT

LOVE said, "Lie still and think of me,"
　Sleep, "Close your eyes till break of day,"
But Dreams came by and smilingly
　Gave both to Love and Sleep their way.

SONG

When Love comes singing to his heart
  That would not wake for me,
I think that I shall know his joy
  By my own ecstasy.

And though the sea were all between,
  The time their hands shall meet,
My heart will know his happiness,
  So wildly it will beat.

And when he bends above her mouth,
  Rejoicing for his sake,
My soul will sing a song, but oh,
  My heart will break.

THE KISS

I HOPED that he would love me,
  And he has kissed my mouth,
But I am like a stricken bird
  That cannot reach the south.

For though I know he loves me,
  To-night my heart is sad;
His kiss was not so wonderful
  As all the dreams I had.

NOVEMBER

THE world is tired, the year is old,
   The faded leaves are glad to die,
The wind goes shivering with cold
   Among the rushes dry.

Our love is dying like the grass,
   And we who kissed grow coldly kind,
Half glad to see our poor love pass
   Like leaves along the wind.

THE WIND

A WIND is blowing over my soul,
   I hear it cry the whole night through—
Is there no peace for me on earth
   Except with you?

Alas, the wind has made me wise,
   Over my naked soul it blew,—
There is no peace for me on earth
   Even with you.

A WINTER NIGHT

My window-pane is starred with frost,
  The world is bitter cold to-night,
The moon is cruel and the wind
  Is like a two-edged sword to smite.

God pity all the homeless ones,
  The beggars pacing to and fro,
God pity all the poor to-night
  Who walk the lamp-lit streets of snow.

My room is like a bit of June,
  Warm and close-curtained fold on fold,
But somewhere, like a homeless child,
  My heart is crying in the cold.

THE METROPOLITAN TOWER

WE walked together in the dusk
  To watch the tower grow dimly white,
And saw it lift against the sky
  Its flower of amber light.

You talked of half a hundred things,
  I kept each hurried word you said;
And when at last the hour was full,
  I saw the light turn red.

You did not know the time had come,
  You did not see the sudden flower,
Nor know that in my heart Love's birth
  Was reckoned from that hour.

GRAMMERCY PARK

THE little park was filled with peace,
　The walks were carpeted with snow,
But every iron gate was locked,
　Lest if we entered, peace would go.

We circled it a dozen times,
　The wind was blowing from the sea,
I only felt your restless eyes
　Whose love was like a cloak for me.

Oh heavy gates that fate has locked
　To bar the joy we can not win,
Peace would go out forever
　If we should enter in.

IN THE METROPOLITAN MUSEUM

INSIDE the tiny Pantheon
  We stood together silently,
Leaving the restless crowd awhile
  As ships find shelter from the sea.

The ancient centuries came back
  To cover us a moment's space,
And through the dome the light was glad
  Because it shone upon your face.

Ah, not from Rome but farther still,
  Beyond sun-smitten Salamis,
The moment took us, till you leaned
  To find the present with a kiss.

CONEY ISLAND

Why did you bring me here?
The sand is white with snow,
Over the wooden domes
The winter sea-winds blow—
There is no shelter near,
　Come, let us go.

With foam of icy lace
The sea creeps up the sand,
The wind is like a hand
That strikes us in the face.
Doors that June set a-swing
Are bolted long ago;
We try them uselessly—
Alas, there cannot be
For us a second spring;
　Come, let us go.

UNION SQUARE

WITH the man I love who loves me not,
  I walked in the street-lamps' flare;
We watched the world go home that night
  In a flood through Union Square.

I leaned to catch the words he said
  That were light as a snowflake falling;
Ah well that he never leaned to hear
  The words my heart was calling.

And on we walked and on we walked
  Past the fiery lights of the picture shows—
Where the girls with thirsty eyes go by
  On the errand each man knows.

And on we walked and on we walked,
  At the door at last we said good-bye;
I knew by his smile he had not heard
  My heart's unuttered cry.

With the man I love who loves me not
  I walked in the street-lamps' flare—
But oh, the girls who ask for love
  In the lights of Union Square.

CENTRAL PARK AT DUSK

BUILDINGS above the leafless trees
  Loom high as castles in a dream,
While one by one the lamps come out
  To thread the twilight with a gleam.

There is no sign of leaf or bud,
  A hush is over everything—
Silent as women wait for love,
  The world is waiting for the spring.

YOUNG LOVE

I

I CANNOT heed the words they say,
  The lights grow far away and dim,
Amid the laughing girls and men
  My eyes unbidden seek for him.

I hope that when he smiles at me
  He does not guess my joy and pain,
For if he did, he is too kind
  To ever look my way again.

II

I have a secret in my heart
  No one has ever heard,
And still it sings there day by day
  A caged and restless bird.

And though it beats against the bars,
  I do not set it free,
For I am happier to know
  It only sings for me.

III

I wrote his name along the beach,
  I love the letters so.

YOUNG LOVE

Far up it seemed and out of reach,
  For still the tide was low.

But, oh, the sea came creeping up,
  And washed the name away,
And on the sand where it had been
  A bit of sea-grass lay.

A bit of sea-grass on the sand,
  Dropped from a mermaid's hair—
Oh, had she come to kiss his name
  And leave a token there?

IV

What am I that he should love me,
He who stands so far above me,
  What am I?
I am like a cowslip turning
  Toward the sky,
Where a planet's golden burning
Breaks the cowslip's heart with yearning,
What am I that he should love me,
  What am I?

V

O dreams that flock about my sleep,
  I pray you bring my love to me,
And let me think I hear his voice
  Again ring free.

YOUNG LOVE

And if you care to please me well,
  And live to-morrow in my mind,
Let him who was so cold before,
  To-night seem kind.

VI

I plucked a daisy in the fields,
  And there beneath the sun
I let its silver petals fall
  One after one.

I said, "He loves me, loves me not,"
  And oh, my heart beat fast,
The flower was kind, it let me say
  "He loves me," last.

I kissed the drooping, leafless stem,
  But oh, my poor heart knew
The words the flower had said to me,
  They were not true.

VII

I sent my love a letter,
  And if he loves me not,
He shall not find my love for him
  In any line or dot.

But if he loves me truly,
  He'll find it hidden deep,
As dawn gleams red through chilly clouds
  To eyes awaked from sleep.

VIII

The world is cold and gray and wet,
And I am heavy-hearted, yet
When I am home and look to see
The place my letters wait for me,
If I should find *one* letter there,
I think I should not greatly care
If it were rainy or were fair,
For all the world would suddenly
Seem like a festival to me.

IX

Across the twilight's violet
  His curtained window glimmers gold;
Oh happy light that round my love
    Can fold.

Oh happy book within his hand,
  Oh happy page he glorifies,
Oh happy little word beneath
    His eyes.

But oh, thrice happy, happy I
  Who love him more than songs can tell,
For in the heaven of his heart
    I dwell.

SONNETS AND LYRICS

PRIMAVERA MIA

As kings, seeing their lives about to pass,
Take off the heavy ermine and the crown,
So had the trees that autumn-time laid down
Their golden garments on the dying grass,
When I, who watched the seasons in the glass
Of my own thoughts, saw all the autumn's brown
Leap into life and wear a sunny gown
Of leafage fresh as happy April has.
Great spring came singing upward from the south;
For in my heart, far carried on the wind,
Your words like wingèd seeds took root and grew,
And all the world caught music from your mouth;
I saw the light as one who had been blind,
And knew my sun and song and spring were you.

FOR THE ANNIVERSARY OF JOHN KEATS' DEATH

(February 23, 1821)

At midnight, when the moonlit cypress trees
Have woven round his grave a magic shade,
Still weeping the unfinished hymn he made,
There moves fresh Maia, like a morning breeze
Blown over jonquil beds when warm rains cease.
And stooping where her poet's head is laid,
Selene weeps, while all the tides are stayed,
And swaying seas are darkened into peace.
But they who wake the meadows and the tides
Have hearts too kind to bid him wake from sleep,
Who murmurs sometimes when his dreams are deep,
Startling the Quiet Land where he abides,
And charming still, sad-eyed Persephone
With visions of the sunny earth and sea.

SILENCE

(To Eleonora Duse)

WE are anhungered after solitude,
Deep stillness pure of any speech or sound,
Soft quiet hovering over pools profound,
The silences that on the desert brood,
Above a windless hush of empty seas,
The broad unfurling banners of the dawn;
A faëry forest where there sleeps a Faun;
Our souls are sick for solitudes like these.
O woman who divined our weariness,
And set the crown of silence on your art,
From what undreamed-of depth within your heart
Have you sent forth the hush that makes us free
To hear an instant, high above earth's stress,
The shadowy music of infinity?

FEAR

I AM afraid, oh, I am so afraid!
The cold black fear is clutching me to-night
As long ago when they would take the light
And leave the little child who would have prayed,
Frozen and sleepless at the thought of death.
My heart that beats too fast will rest too soon;
I shall not know if it be night or noon—
Yet shall I struggle in the dark for breath?
Will no one fight the Terror for my sake,
The heavy darkness that no dawn will break?
How can they leave me in that dark alone,
Who loved the joy of light and warmth so much,
And thrilled so with the sense of sound and touch—
How can they shut me underneath a stone?

GALAHAD IN THE CASTLE OF THE MAIDENS

(To the maiden with the hidden face in Abbey's painting)

THE other maidens raised their eyes to him
Who stumbled in before them when the fight
Had left him victor, with a victor's right.
I think his eyes with quick hot tears grew dim;
He scarcely saw her swaying white and slim,
And trembling slightly, dreaming of his might,
Nor knew he touched her hand, as cool and light
As a wan wraith's beside a river's rim.
The other maidens raised their eyes to see
And only she has hid her face away,
And yet I think she loved him more than they,
And very fairly fashioned was her face.
Yet for Love's shame and sweet humility,
She could not meet him with their queenlike grace.

TO AN ÆOLIAN HARP

THE winds have grown articulate in thee,
And voiced again the wail of ancient woe
That smote upon the winds of long ago;
The cries of Trojan women as they flee,
The quivering moan of pale Andromache,
Now lifted loud with pain and now brought low.
It is the soul of sorrow that we know,
As in a shell the soul of all the sea.
So sometimes in the compass of a song,
Unknown to him who sings, through lips that live,
The voiceless dead of long-forgotten lands
Proclaim to us their heaviness and wrong
In sweeping sadness of the winds that give
Thy strings no rest from weariless wild hands.

TO ERINNA

Was Time not harsh to you, or was he kind,
O pale Erinna of the perfect lyre,
That he has left no word of singing fire
Whereby you waked the dreaming Lesbian wind,
And kindled night along the darkened shore?
O girl whose lips Erato stooped to kiss,
Do you go sorrowing because of this
In fields where poets sing forevermore?
Or are you glad, and is it best to be
A silent music men have never heard,
A dream in all our hearts that we may say:
"Her voice had all the rapture of the sea,
And all the clear cool quiver of a bird
Deep in a forest at the break of day"?

TO CLEÏS

(The daughter of Sappho)

WHEN the dusk was wet with dew,
  Cleïs, did the muses nine
  Listen in a silent line
While your mother sang to you?

Did they weep or did they smile
  When she crooned to still your cries,
  She, a muse in human guise,
Who forsook her lyre awhile?

Did you feel her wild heart beat?
  Did the warmth of all the sun
  Through your little body run
When she kissed your hands and feet?

Did your fingers, babywise,
  Touch her face and touch her hair,
  Did you think your mother fair,
Could you bear her burning eyes?

Are the songs that soothed your fears
  Vanished like a vanished flame,
  Save the line where shines your name
Starlike down the graying years? . . .

TO CLEÏS

Cleïs speaks no word to me,
  For the land where she has gone
  Lies as still at dusk and dawn
As a windless, tideless sea.

PARIS IN SPRING

THE city 's all a-shining
  Beneath a fickle sun,
A gay young wind 's a-blowing,
  The little shower is done.
But the rain-drops still are clinging
  And falling one by one—
Oh, it 's Paris, it 's Paris,
  And spring-time has begun.

I know the Bois is twinkling
  In a sort of hazy sheen,
And down the Champs the gray old arch
  Stands cold and still between.
But the walk is flecked with sunlight
  Where the great acacias lean,
Oh, it 's Paris, it 's Paris,
  And the leaves are growing green.

The sun 's gone in, the sparkle 's dead,
  There falls a dash of rain,
But who would care when such an air
  Comes blowing up the Seine?

[90]

PARIS IN SPRING

And still Ninette sits sewing
  Beside her window-pane,
When it 's Paris, it 's Paris,
  And spring-time 's come again.

MADEIRA FROM THE SEA

Out of the delicate dream of the distance an emerald
    emerges
Veiled in the violet folds of the air of the sea;
Softly the dream grows awakening—shimmering
    white of a city,
Splashes of crimson, the gay bougainvillea, the palms.
High in the infinite blue of its heaven a quiet cloud
    lingers,
Lost and forgotten by winds that have fallen asleep,
Fallen asleep to the tune of a Portuguese song in a
    garden.

CITY VIGNETTES

I

DAWN

THE greenish sky glows up in misty reds,
  The purple shadows turn to brick and stone,
The dreams wear thin, men turn upon their beds,
  And hear the milk-cart jangle by alone.

II

DUSK

The city's street, a roaring, blackened stream,
  Walled in by granite, through whose thousand eyes
A thousand yellow lights begin to gleam,
  And over all the pale, untroubled skies.

III

RAIN AT NIGHT

The street-lamps shine in a yellow line
  Down the splashy, gleaming street,
And the rain is heard, now loud, now blurred
  By the tread of homing feet.

BY THE SEA

BESIDE an ebbing northern sea,
While stars awaken one by one,
We walk together, I and he.

He woos me with an easy grace
That proves him only half sincere;
A light smile flickers on his face.

To him love-making is an art,
And as a flutist plays a flute,
So does he play upon his heart

A music varied to his whim.
He has no use for love of mine,
He would not have me answer him.

To hide my eyes within the night
I watch the changeful lighthouse gleam
Alternately with red and white.

My laughter smites upon my ears,
So one who cries and wakes from sleep
Knows not it is himself he hears.

[94]

BY THE SEA

What if my voice should let him know
The mocking words were all a sham,
And lips that laugh could tremble so?

What if I lost the power to lie,
And he should only hear his name
In a low, broken cry?

TRIOLETS

I

Love looked back as he took his flight,
  And lo, his eyes were filled with tears.
Was it for love of lost delight
Love looked back as he took his flight?
Only I know while day grew night,
  Turning still to the vanished years,
Love looked back as he took his flight,
  And lo, his eyes were filled with tears.

II

(Written in a copy of "La Vita Nuova." For M. C. S.)

If you were Lady Beatrice
  And I the Florentine,
I'd never waste my time like this—
If you were Lady Beatrice
I'd woo and then demand a kiss,
  Nor weep like Dante here, I ween,
If you were Lady Beatrice
  And I the Florentine.

[96]

TRIOLETS

III

(Written in a copy of ''The Poems of Sappho.'')

Beyond the dim Hesperides,
  The girl who sang them long ago
Could never dream that over seas,
Beyond the dim Hesperides,
The wind would blow such songs as these—
  I wonder now if she can know,
Beyond the dim Hesperides,
  The girl who sang them long ago?

IV

Dead leaves upon the stream
  And dead leaves on the air—
All of my lost hopes seem
Dead leaves upon the stream;
I watch them in a dream,
  Going, I know not where,
Dead leaves upon the stream
  And dead leaves on the air.

VOX CORPORIS

THE beast to the beast is calling,
  And the mind bends down to wait;
Like the stealthy lord of the jungle,
  The man calls to his mate.

The beast to the beast is calling,
  They rush through the twilight sweet—
But the mind is a wary hunter;
  He will not let them meet.

A BALLAD OF TWO KNIGHTS

Two knights rode forth at early dawn
  A-seeking maids to wed;
Said one, "My lady must be fair,
  With gold hair on her head."

Then spoke the other knight-at-arms:
  "I care not for her face,
But she I love must be a dove
  For purity and grace."

And each knight blew upon his horn
  And went his separate way,
And each knight found a lady-love
  Before the fall of day.

But she was brown who should have had
  The shining yellow hair—
The knights had both forgot their words
  Or else they ceased to care;

For he who wanted purity
  Brought home a wanton wild—
And when each saw the other knight
  I think that each knight smiled.

CHRISTMAS CAROL

THE kings they came from out the south,
    All dressed in ermine fine;
They bore Him gold and chrysoprase,
    And gifts of precious wine.

The shepherds came from out the north,
    Their coats were brown and old;
They brought Him little new-born lambs—
    They had not any gold.

The wise men came from out the east,
    And they were wrapped in white;
The star that led them all the way
    Did glorify the night.

The angels came from heaven high,
    And they were clad with wings;
And lo, they brought a joyful song
    The host of heaven sings.

The kings they knocked upon the door,
    The wise men entered in,
The shepherds followed after them
    To hear the song begin.

CHRISTMAS CAROL

The angels sang through all the night
Until the rising sun,
But little Jesus fell asleep
Before the song was done.

THE FAËRY FOREST

THE faëry forest glimmered
  Beneath an ivory moon,
The silver grasses shimmered
  Against a faëry tune.

Beneath the silken silence
  The crystal branches slept,
And dreaming through the dew-fall
  The cold, white blossoms wept.

A FANTASY

HER voice is like clear water
  That drips upon a stone
In forests far and silent
  Where Quiet plays alone.

Her thoughts are like the lotus
  Abloom by sacred streams
Beneath the temple arches
  Where Quiet sits and dreams.

Her kisses are the roses
  That glow while dusk is deep
In Persian garden closes
  Where Quiet falls asleep.

A MINUET OF MOZART'S

Across the dimly lighted room
  The violin drew wefts of sound;
  Airily they wove and wound
And glimmered gold against the gloom.

I watched the music turn to light,
  But at the pausing of the bow,
  The web was broken, and the glow
Was drowned within the wave of night.

TWILIGHT

Dreamily, over the roofs,
   The cold spring rain is falling;
Out in the lonely tree
   A bird is calling, calling.

Slowly, over the earth,
   The wings of night are falling;
My heart, like the bird in the tree,
   Is calling, calling, calling.